Doll Hospital™

Saving Marissa

♥ ♥ ♥ ♥ ♥

Doll Hospital™

Saving Marissa

♥ ♥ ♥ ♥ ♥

BY JOAN HOLUB

Illustrations by Ann Iosa

A LITTLE APPLE PAPERBACK

SCHOLASTIC INC.

New York   Toronto   London   Auckland   Sydney
Mexico City   New Delhi   Hong Kong   Buenos Aires

ISBN 0-439-40181-X

Design by Steve Scott

12 11 10 9 8 7 6 5 4 3 2 1   3 4 5 6 7 8/0
40

Printed in the U.S.A.
First printing, July 2003

For Joy Peskin,
who thought of doll hospitals.

With thanks to
Phyllis and her baby doll Linda
and to
my mom for taking
my doll Annie and me to a doll hospital.

— J.H.

Table of Contents

Doll Hospital™

Saving Marissa

CHAPTER 1
Little Kids

♥ ♥ ♥ ♥ ♥

Rose hid her face in her hands. "If anybody finds out I spent today at day care, I'll die." She didn't budge from the backseat of the van. Neither did her little sister, Lila.

Their grandmother opened the van's front door and stepped out onto the driveway. "I'm sorry, but it's the best I could do on short notice. I forgot your school is closed today for teacher meetings. And I'd already made plans to go out."

Lila stared at the house where they'd parked. "*This* is the day care? It looks like a normal house. Except for the sign out front that says Doodle Dandy Day Care."

"What did you expect?" asked their grandmother. She opened the van's back door for Rose and Lila.

Lila shrugged. "More baby stuff, I guess." She grabbed her beagle-shaped backpack, hopped out of the van, and headed for the front porch.

Rose checked inside her backpack for her books and

other things she needed. Her fingers touched something soft and fuzzy. Her good-luck charm.

The key chains clipped to Rose's backpack clinked together as she went up the sidewalk. She tried one last time to change her grandmother's mind. "Let's go back home. I can take care of Lila and me for one measly day."

Her grandmother didn't answer. Her long tie-dyed skirt swirled as she hurried after Lila.

Rose followed them up the steps to the porch, not quite stomping. But almost. "I'm ten — not two. I'm too old for a baby-sitter," she insisted.

"You're both too young to stay home on your own," said her grandmother.

"Besides, this isn't a baby-sitter. It's day care," said Lila.

Rose rolled her eyes. "Don't remind me."

Lila rang the doorbell. The chimes played the "Rock-a-bye Baby" song. Lila hummed along.

Rose groaned.

Inside the house, footsteps thundered closer.

"Man!" said their grandmother. "Sounds like a herd of buffalo in there."

"Buffalo babies, probably," said Rose.

The door opened, and a smiling woman with short gray hair greeted them. She wore blue pants decorated with numbers and a shirt covered with the ABC's.

A little girl with red hair peeked around one side of the woman. She held up three fingers. "I'm fwee!" she told them.

A twin red-haired boy squeezed past on the woman's other side. He stopped sucking his thumb and pointed at Rose and Lila. "Big kids," he said.

"Hi. I phoned a few minutes ago about bringing my granddaughters over for the day," their grandmother explained.

"Oh, yes! Come on in," said the woman. She gently guided the boy and girl away from the door and back down the hall.

"These are my granddaughters, Rose and Lila," said their grandmother. She nudged the girls ahead of her into the house.

"You can call me Ms. Jill. All the other kids do," the woman told Rose and Lila over her shoulder. "And these two little ones are Beth and Bryan."

Ms. Jill led them to a living room. Beth and Bryan dashed into the next room, where four other toddlers were playing.

"Thanks for watching the girls today," their grandmother said. She had to talk loudly to be heard over the noise the little kids were making nearby. "I know you normally just take preschoolers and kindergartners. But I couldn't find a baby-sitter, and I was getting desperate."

"No problem. I only have six children on Tuesdays, so now we'll make eight. The more, the merrier!" Ms. Jill smiled at Rose and Lila as though she was really delighted to see them. They smiled back. Ms. Jill was so nice, it was hard not to.

The phone rang.

Bryan ran in, climbed on a chair, and answered it. "Hewwo," he said.

"Excuse me a minute," said Ms. Jill.

"I need to get going now in any case." Their grandmother waved good-bye to Ms. Jill and went toward the front door. Rose and Lila trailed after her.

Behind them, they heard Ms. Jill talking to Bryan. "This is a grown-up phone. Why don't you play with this toy phone instead?"

"Where are you going today, anyway?" Lila asked their grandmother.

"And why can't we go with you?" added Rose.

They had tried to ask these questions on the drive over. But their grandmother had been in too much of a hurry to answer.

"It's business," said their grandmother. She smoothed her long gray braid with one hand and jiggled her bead necklaces with the other. A sure sign she was nervous.

Rose squinted up at her. "What kind?"

"The grown-up kind," said their grandmother. "I'd

better run. I've got to be there by nine-thirty. So I'll be signing off now."

Rose and Lila looked at each other. "Signing off?" they echoed. Their grandmother never said good-bye like that.

All of a sudden, Beth came along and wrapped her arms around Rose's knees. She looked up at Rose with big brown eyes. "I'm fwee," she announced.

"I'll be back for you girls at four," their grandmother promised. Then the front door whooshed shut behind her.

Rose stared down at the girl hugging her knees. "If we make it that long."

CHAPTER 2
Baby-sitting

♥　♥　♥　♥　♥

Rose gave up trying to peel Beth from her knees. "This kid must be part boa constrictor," she said.

When they heard Bryan giggling in the other room, Beth let go and dashed toward the sound.

"Far Nana is up to something," said Lila.

Far Nana was the nickname they'd given their grandmother five years ago, when Rose was five and Lila was three. It was because she lived far away from their apartment back in the city.

Rose and Lila were living with her for a year while their parents were in Africa. Their mom and dad were doctors. The African villages where they were working weren't safe enough for Rose and Lila. So the girls had to stay behind in America at Far Nana's.

"Yeah. No kidding," said Rose. She bent down to check her knees for drool.

"Where do you think she —?" began Lila.

Just then Ms. Jill returned. Her smile was sagging. "That was my assistant on the phone. She's got a cold and won't be able to come in. Looks like it's going to be just us big kids and the little ones today."

"We'll be your assistants," Lila offered.

"You will?" asked Ms. Jill.

"We will?" asked Rose at the same time.

Lila nodded yes. "I want to learn how to baby-sit."

"What a great idea!" said Ms. Jill, smiling again. "The kids will love playing with you. I have lots of activities planned for today, so I can use your help. Go on into the playroom. I'll be there in a jiff."

Rose and Lila hung their backpacks on hooks in the playroom and looked around. Two little kids were on the floor, playing with building blocks. Two others were coloring. Beth and Bryan were playing tag.

Lila pulled a purple dinosaur from a basket full of stuffed animals. "This is more like it," she said.

"Yeah," said Rose. "Now we're baby-sitting, instead of being baby-sat."

"No, I mean, look at all the cool things in here," said Lila. She waved a hand toward the toys scattered around the room. A big plastic playhouse shaped like a castle stood against one wall.

Lila dropped the dinosaur. She picked up a toy crown with fake jewels and put it on her head.

"Since when do you like baby stuff so much, Your Highness?" asked Rose.

"Since today. Someday I'll be queen of the baby-sitters, and I'll get rich!" said Lila.

Out of the corner of her eye, Rose saw Bryan try to grab the key chains off her backpack. "Hey! Those are for big kids." She rushed over to stop him. He wiggled around her and tried to grab them again. Rose shooed him away.

"I don't think baby-sitting is all that easy," she told Lila as she wrestled with Bryan.

"Sure it is. All you have to do is say stuff like 'No hitting. No biting.' And 'Into the time-out chair, you bad kids!'" said Lila.

Rose rolled her eyes. "We'll see," she said.

CHAPTER 3
Napping

♥ ♥ ♥ ♥ ♥

"Simon says: Quack like a duck," said Rose.

Six little kids and one eight-year-old quacked.

"Simon says: Meow like a cat," said Rose.

Six little kids and one eight-year-old meowed.

"Bark like a dog," said Rose.

One eight-year-old barked. Six little kids giggled.

"Oops!" Lila covered her mouth, embarrassed. "I take it back."

"Simon says: No take-backs," said Rose.

"Simon says: It's nap time!" called Ms. Jill.

Rose and Lila helped the kids lie on their mats on the playroom floor. They took turns reading picture books aloud until the kids looked sleepy.

Then they tiptoed into the kitchen, sat at the table, and watched Ms. Jill wash child-sized dishes.

"You'd better sit down and rest," Lila told her. "Before those kids wake up again."

Rose rested her chin in one hand and yawned. "Yeah. I need a nap, too. Those kids wore me out."

Ms. Jill smiled. "I love having children in the house. I never had any of my own. Besides, nap time is when I get ready for the afternoon activities. When they wake up, we're going to bake gingerbread cookies."

"Yum!" said Lila.

"That reminds me: I'll need my cookie cookbook from the den," said Ms. Jill. "It's an old family cookbook, so I put it on the top shelf of my bookcase for safekeeping."

"We'll get it," said Lila. "I love gingerbread cookies." She stood up and dragged Rose from the chair.

"You love any cookies," said Rose.

"Thanks," Ms. Jill called softly after them. "The den is at the end of the hall, past the stairs. Look for a big blue-and-white book with a gingerbread man on the front."

"Gotcha," said Lila. She tugged Rose down the hall.

When they got to the den, Rose unlatched the baby gate blocking the doorway, and they went in.

CHAPTER 4
Snooping

♥ ♥ ♥ ♥ ♥

One wall of the den was filled with bookshelves. A desk and chair sat against the other wall. The rest of the room was filled with storage boxes, pictures, and knickknacks.

Lila's eyes sparkled when she saw what was on the desk. "Cool! Ms. Jill has a computer!"

"Everybody has a computer, except Far Nana," said Rose.

Lila jiggled the computer mouse, but the screen didn't light up. "Rats. It's off."

Rose stood on a step stool, found the cookie cookbook on the top shelf, and pulled it out. Lila began nosing around the room, checking things out.

"Look at this cool poster of a movie called *It Came from Outer Space*. And this old *Lassie* lunch box," she said.

Rose poked around, too. "This record player has an Elvis Presley record on it. Ms. Jill's stuff looks even more old-timey than Far Nana's hippie junk."

"Yeah. Watch me do this Hula Hoop!" Lila put a big green hoop around her waist. She wiggled her hips and tried to make it go around.

The hoop wobbled. It bobbled. Lila got dizzy and accidentally knocked a box off a shelf and onto the floor.

"Oops." She stopped Hula Hooping and looked down at the mess she'd made.

Little dresses in different styles and colors were scattered on the rug. Each was on a small hanger.

"Lila!" Rose scolded in her big-sister voice. "Help me pick this stuff up."

Together, they gathered the dresses, admiring each one as they replaced it in the box. There were pale linen gowns with pleats, tucks, and pearl buttons. There were flowered cotton gowns with colorful stitching. And there were dresses decorated with dainty lace trim and satin ribbon.

Lila picked up some other things that had fallen out of the box. "Look! A baby bottle. And a brush and mirror. This stuff is so teeny!" She held the small mirror close to her face so it reflected one of her green eyes.

Rose held up a tiny pair of knitted booties. "Yeah. These dresses and shoes are too little for a girl or even a baby. I think they're doll clothes."

"Where's the doll?" asked Lila, looking around.

Rose spied a doll-sized carriage in a corner of the

room. One wheel was broken, so it was leaning over. "Maybe in there?" she guessed, pointing.

They went over to the white wicker buggy and looked in. It was filled with frilly blankets. Rose pushed them aside, uncovering a pale pink face with very short golden curls.

"Oh! A baby doll," said Lila. "It's so cute!"

"Too bad somebody drew on it, though." Rose rubbed a finger against the colorful scribbles on the doll's cheeks. "It doesn't come off."

The doll in the buggy wore a ruffled bonnet and a pink dress embroidered with flowers. Eyelet lace threaded with ribbon was sewn around the hem.

"I think those dresses belong to this doll," said Rose.

"But Ms. Jill doesn't have any kids. So whose doll is this?" wondered Lila.

"She's mine," said a grown-up voice behind them.

Rose and Lila turned around. Ms. Jill stood in the doorway.

"Uh-oh," said Lila.

"Sorry we snooped," said Rose.

"That's okay," Ms. Jill said. She came inside and knelt beside the doll buggy. She lifted the doll out so Rose and Lila could see her better. "Her name's Marissa."

"Did you get her when you were a kid, or after you grew up?" asked Lila.

"My aunt bought her for me when I was eight," said Ms. Jill. "Marissa was beautiful then. And she used to be able to talk when this string was pulled."

Ms. Jill turned Marissa around so Rose and Lila could see the string coming out of the doll's back.

"Cool," said Lila.

"Yes," said Ms. Jill. "But that was a long time ago." She sighed and put the doll back in its buggy.

"What happened to her?" asked Rose.

Ms. Jill looked sad as she tucked the lacy blanket around the doll. "I didn't take care of her as well as I should have."

"Far Nana could fix her, I bet," said Lila. "She has a doll hospital in her house. She's a doctor, like our parents. Only she fixes dolls, and our parents fix people."

Ms. Jill looked hopeful. "Do you really think your grandmother could make her talk again?"

Rose and Lila shared a secret sister look.

"Definitely," said Rose. "She's good at that."

CHAPTER 5
Visitors

♥ ♥ ♥ ♥ ♥

The doorbell rang a few minutes before four that afternoon. It was Far Nana.

"Hi! Ms. Jill has a doll you need to fix," Lila informed her, first thing. She pulled their grandmother inside and down the hall without giving her a chance to speak.

"The girls said you might be able to repair my Marissa," Ms. Jill told Far Nana. "But only if you have time." She followed Lila and Far Nana into the den.

"I'll get our stuff," Rose called after them.

On her way into the playroom, she stumbled over her backpack. It was lying open on the floor. Her things had spilled out of it.

"How did this get on the floor?" she wondered aloud.

She picked up her bag and checked through her stuff. Cold, worried prickles went down her spine. Something was missing — her lucky charm!

Bryan giggled. Rose frowned at him. He was holding a small gray stuffed toy with a blue ribbon around its neck. The fuzzy bunny had a cute pink nose, long ears, and a puffy white tail. It looked familiar.

"BB!" shouted Rose. She dropped her backpack and chased Bryan.

Ms. Jill hurried into the playroom when she heard Rose yell. Lila was close behind her.

"Who's BB?" Ms. Jill asked in surprise.

"It's short for Bunny Boo," Lila said. "That's Rose's favorite stuffed animal from when she was a baby. I guess Bryan got it from her backpack."

"Bryan! Give that bunny back to Rose! It's *her* toy," Ms. Jill said in a firm voice.

Bryan ran down the hall, laughing even more. Rose kept chasing. Ms. Jill and Lila hurried after them.

Rose caught up with Bryan by the front door. She snatched at the bunny, and they played tug-of-war with it.

"Give me my —" Rose began.

The front door opened and Bryan let go.

"— Bunny Boo!" Rose finished.

A boy Rose's age came in the door just in time to hear.

Rose tumbled backward onto the floor, holding BB by one ear. She stared up at the boy in horror.

Bryan popped his thumb in his mouth. He leaned against the boy as though he knew him.

"Hello, Bart," Ms. Jill said to the new arrival.

"Hi," said Bart. But he was looking at Rose's bunny. She jumped to her feet and hid it behind her back.

Bart nudged Bryan. "C'mon. Mom's waiting out front for us."

Bryan ran out the door. Outside, a woman got out of a blue car parked along the street. She waved at Ms. Jill through the open front door. Rose could see two car seats for little kids in the backseat of the car.

"Beth!" Ms. Jill called. "Your mom's here!"

Beth came running from the playroom. She hugged Rose's knees on her way to the front door. She smiled with grape-juice-stained lips. "Bye, Wose."

"Bye, boa-girl," Rose said weakly.

Beth let go of Rose's knees and held Bart's hand.

Bart snickered back at Rose as he led his sister outside. "See you, *Wose*."

Rose and Lila watched him get into his mom's car with Beth and Bryan.

"Isn't that boy in your class at school?" asked Lila.

Rose nodded. "His name is Bart. And he saw me here, at day care! So now I can officially die of embarrassment."

"Uh-oh!" said Lila.

As the blue car drove away, Bart grinned at them through the window.

Just then, Far Nana came into the front hallway, carrying Ms. Jill's doll in its buggy. She looked happy, like she always did when someone gave her a doll to repair.

"So, how was your day?" she asked Rose and Lila.

"Great," said Rose. She wiped little-kid slobber off her bunny with a tissue. "Just great."

CHAPTER 6

Repairs

♥ ♥ ♥ ♥ ♥

Back at their grandmother's house, they all carried things in from the van. Lila carried the leftovers from the early dinner they'd eaten at the Joy of Soy Café. Far Nana carried Ms. Jill's doll and buggy.

Rose carried Far Nana's bag. A book fell out of it onto the grass, and Rose picked it up. Far Nana grabbed it before she could read the title.

"What's that?" asked Rose.

"Don't ask. I'll tell you when I'm ready," said Far Nana. She looked embarrassed. "Which is *not* now, by the way."

"But —" began Rose.

"Can't I have any secrets around here?" asked Far Nana. She went in the front door.

"Wow! Why's she so cranky?" Lila whispered to Rose on the porch.

Rose shrugged. She was dying to know where Far Nana had gone that day. But she wasn't about to ask again.

After they put everything away, the three of them

climbed upstairs. They went to a turreted room on the third floor where Far Nana had her doll hospital. The room was nicknamed the witch's hat because of its tall, pointed roof.

Doll hospital stuff filled the inside of the witch's hat. Colorful spools of thread, fabric, and ribbons sat on shelves and hung out of drawers. There were boxes and bags of doll parts like eyeballs, shoes, and wigs. There were lots of dolls, too: big dolls, little dolls, and in-between-sized dolls.

Far Nana set Ms. Jill's doll buggy on her worktable and lifted Marissa out. She turned the doll around and around, admiring it.

Rose and Lila stood on either side of their grandmother, studying the doll.

"I wanted a doll like this when I was a girl, but they were too expensive," said Far Nana. "This doll can do just about everything."

"Does it dance?" asked Rose.

"Well, no," said Far Nana.

"Sing?" asked Lila.

Far Nana frowned at them. "No."

"Then what?" asked Lila.

"Besides talk," added Rose.

"It wets and drinks, and its eyes open and shut. Back in the 1950s, that was pretty cool stuff for a doll to do," said Far Nana.

"Can you get those marks off its face?" asked Rose.

"Depends on what made them," said Far Nana. She peered at the marks over the top of her glasses. "Some inks will come off. Some won't."

"Can you make her talk again?" asked Lila. "I think that's what matters most to Ms. Jill."

"Probably. I've repaired lots of talking dolls," said Far Nana. "But that will have to wait until I can buy a new voice box. There is one thing I think I can fix tonight, though."

She set the doll aside and pulled some tools from a drawer. Then she began working on the broken buggy wheel.

A few minutes later, the wheel was spinning on the buggy, good as new.

"That's one task down," said Far Nana.

"So can we hear Marissa's story now?" Rose asked hopefully.

"Yeah, please don't make us wait till tomorrow," begged Lila.

After they'd come to live with Far Nana, Rose and Lila had discovered something amazing. Far Nana could talk to dolls! She could hear dolls' thoughts and tell their stories. At first, Rose and Lila hadn't believed it. But the dolls' stories sounded so real that, by now, they were pretty sure it was true.

Far Nana checked the doll-shaped clock hanging on

the wall. "I guess there's enough time. Let's try it and see." She put the baby doll in its buggy, sitting upright. She tucked the lacy blanket around its shoulders.

Then she sat in her work chair a few feet away. Her four cats were sleeping on the window seat. Lila snuggled in with them.

Rose turned off the overhead light and clicked on Far Nana's Lava lamp. She unwrapped a plate of gingerbread cookies Ms. Jill had given them before they left. She handed some to Lila and Far Nana and took two for herself. Then she sat cross-legged in the big wicker chair with the high, round back.

And they waited.

Marissa smiled sweetly at them from within her soft blankets. Her baby-blue eyes sparkled in the lamp's glow.

For a while, cookie munching was the only sound in the witch's hat.

But eventually, Far Nana began to speak. And Marissa began to tell her story.

CHAPTER 7
Giants
Marissa's Story

♥ ♥ ♥ ♥ ♥

The giants are back, whispered the doll in the crib next to mine.

I stopped trying to grab the toys dangling over my head. The bear, horse, and elephant would have to wait. Somehow I knew I had to be still when the giants came. I was pretty smart for a doll just one day old.

There were five of us dolls in the glass window. Five cribs in a row.

We each wore a different nightgown. There was yellow-gown, white-gown, green-gown, blue-gown. And me: pink-gown.

My ruffly bonnet had tiny pink flowers. It scratched my ears. But it was pretty. My booties were cuddly and warm. They had shiny white ribbons.

A sign hung above our cribs. It said: ADOPT-A-BABY-DOLL STORE.

Giants stood on the other side of the window. They smiled. They giggled. They pointed.

Who are they? I whispered.

Girls, said the bear that dangled above me, just out of reach.

What do they want? blue-gown asked from beside me.

Dolls, said the dangle bear.

The girls pressed their noses and hands against the window.

One of them spoke. "I want the one in the blue nightgown. She's so sweet. I could just eat her up!"

They're going to eat us! cried blue-gown.

They are? I asked, getting scared.

Girls don't eat dolls. That just means she likes you, said the dangle horse.

They want to give you names and take you home, said the dangle elephant.

Then one of the girls pointed at me! "I like that one. She's so cute!"

Shessocute? Was that my new name? I wondered.

The big hands picked me up.

My eyes shut. I couldn't open them!

Don't drop me! I said.

The big hands didn't drop me. They gave me to other, smaller hands.

The new hands tilted my head up. My eyes opened again. I was in the main part of the store now. A girl was holding me.

She had short ponytails high on each side of her head. There were light brown polka dots on her cheeks. The girl had legs and arms. Just like mine, only longer.

"She has blue eyes and blond hair, like me," said the polka-dotted girl. "Her eyes open when you tilt her up and close when she lies down." The girl rocked me back and forth. My eyes shut and then opened again.

Another, smaller girl leaned close. She had a stuffed bear in one hand and a lollipop in the other. I wanted a lick. But she didn't offer.

She touched my face. Her finger stuck to my cheek and then popped away.

"Don't touch her with sticky hands, Cousin Ellen," said the polka-dot girl.

Cousin Ellen put her sticky hands on the bear instead. "Make her say something, Jill," she told the polka-dot girl.

So the polka-dot girl had a name — Jill. I whispered it over and over in my head. I wanted to remember it.

I felt a gentle tug at the back of my neck.

"Ma-ma."

Who said that? I wondered.

Cousin Ellen giggled. "Do it again!"

I felt another tug.

"*Ma-ma.*"

It was me! I was the one who'd said it. Only one day old, and already I could speak. I must be some kind of super baby doll!

CHAPTER 8
Getting Adopted
Marissa's Story

♥ ♥ ♥ ♥ ♥

Is she the one you want?" someone asked Jill. It was a grown-up lady wearing a wide skirt. There was an interesting feather in her hat.

Jill smiled at me. "Yes. I want her, Aunt Alice." Then she made little wrinkles in her forehead. "But what's Mother going to say if I bring her home? You know how she feels about dolls."

Aunt Alice puffed an angry sound. Her hat feather wiggled. "Every girl should have a doll."

"My mother didn't," said Jill.

"That's only because we were poor," said Jill's aunt. "But now I can afford to buy a doll."

"And a bear!" added Cousin Ellen.

Aunt Alice smiled. "That's right, dear. And Mr. Fuzzy for my Ellen. The toys are a special treat for our girls' day out."

"Don't worry," she told Jill. "I'll explain to your mother."

31

Aunt Alice turned to another lady. She had a shiny pin on her blouse that said ADOPT-A-BABY-DOLL STORE.

"We'll take this one," Aunt Alice said to her. She gave the lady small pieces of green paper. And little shiny silver buttons. Only they weren't exactly buttons. They had writing and pictures on them.

The store lady handed Jill a big sheet of pink paper. "Fill in your new doll's name on this adoption certificate."

Jill made forehead wrinkles again. "I don't know what to name her."

I have two names already, silly Jilly, I said. *I'm Pinkgown-Shessocute.*

The lady took Jill to a blue rocking chair with flowers painted on it. "Sit in our thinking chair for a few minutes. It's good for thinking of names. Your aunt and I will get the doll's trunk."

Jill rocked me back and forth. The chair creaked. My eyes rocked shut and open. *Creak-tap! Creak-tap!*

She stared at me as she tried out a bunch of names. "Linda, Susan, Tessa, Karen, Jessica . . ."

"I know," said Cousin Ellen. "Your doll and Mr. Fuzzy can get married. Then she can be Mrs. Fuzzy. And I can be the flower girl."

Cousin Ellen pressed the bear's nose against my cheek.

Mr. Fuzzy growled softly.

Grrr, I growled back.

Jill pushed the bear away. "Babies don't get married, Cousin Ellen. Especially not to bears."

Aunt Alice and the store lady came back. Now Jill's aunt was carrying a white baby buggy with wheels.

And the store lady had a box. "Here's your doll's accessory trunk," she told Jill.

Open it! I said to the store lady.

Right then, I found something out. Grown-ups don't listen to baby dolls. The box stayed shut.

"I thought of a name for her," Jill told the store lady. "My two favorite names are Marianne and Melissa. I'm going to put them together and call her Marissa."

"Lovely," said Aunt Alice.

The store lady nodded. "Good. Now we can begin the official adoption."

Jill stopped rocking. She sat up straight.

Cousin Ellen stopped licking her lollipop.

Aunt Alice stood behind the rocking chair.

I knew something important was about to happen.

"Repeat after me," the store lady said to Jill. She read the words on the piece of pink paper out loud. "I promise to take good care of my new baby doll, Marissa."

Jill looked down. She stared straight into my eyes and said, "'I promise to take good care of my new baby doll, Marissa.'"

"Do you promise to feed her when she's hungry? And to change her diaper when she's wet? And to love her forever and ever?" asked the lady.

"Yes," Jill said, very serious. "I promise."

"Excellent!" The store lady handed the pink paper and a pencil to Jill. "Please fill in her name."

Jill wrote the letters M A R I S S A on the paper. Those letters were my very own brand-new name!

The lady wrote the date: June 14, 1956. Then she stamped the paper with two beautiful curlicue words: ADOPTION COMPLETE.

"Smile!" she said. Jill and I smiled.

There was a quick flash of light.

I am pretty brave. But it was a teensy bit scary.

Jill patted me. "It's okay," she cooed. "She just took our picture."

"After it's developed, we'll put your photo in a frame and mail it to you," said the store lady.

Cousin Ellen bounced around in a circle, very excited. "You adopted her, like a real baby! Are you her mama now?"

Jill nodded. "Yes!"

Of course, she's my mama, I said. *Why do you think I said "Ma-ma" when she pulled my talking string?*

Aunt Alice's feather hat dipped near. "Your Marissa is adorable. I can see why you chose her," she told Jill.

She gathered Cousin Ellen and Jill and headed for the door. "Now, let's go home, girls."

Home! Jill was taking me home, just like dangle elephant had said. She carried me to the door.

I called to the other dolls in the window. *Bye-bye, babies. I get to go home with my new mama now! Forever and ever!*

"Bye-bye!" the other baby dolls called back.

"Congratulations! I hope you enjoy your new baby doll," the store lady said to Jill.

Jill grinned back at her. "I will."

She stepped outside and tucked the blanket snug around me. She whispered close to my ear. "I just hope my mother lets me keep you."

CHAPTER 9
A Little More

♥ ♥ ♥ ♥ ♥

Far Nana paused to check the time. The clock-doll's little hand pointed to the eight and its big hand pointed to the twelve.

"We'd better stop," she said. "Tomorrow's a school day."

"Not yet," pleaded Rose. "Just a little more." She didn't even want to think about school yet. Bart would be there.

Lila handed Far Nana another gingerbread cookie. "Pleeeease? With gingerbread icing on top?"

"All right," said Far Nana. "Just a little more."

And Marissa's story continued.

CHAPTER 10

Home

Marissa's Story

♥ ♥ ♥ ♥ ♥

We took a ride. I took a nap.

I heard Jill call, "We're home, Mother."

That woke me up fast. *Yippee! We're home!* I said.

I liked home right away. It was squeaky-clean. There were chairs. And rugs. And pictures on the walls.

The lady named Mother came over to us. She had polka dots on her face, like Jill. But hers had powder on them. She stared at me like I was an ugly bug. "What's that?"

"My new doll," Jill said in a small voice. "Aunt Alice bought her."

Cousin Ellen ducked behind Aunt Alice's wide skirt. She looked a little bit scared of Jill's mother.

I tried to look cute. It did not work.

Mother made an upside-down smile. She didn't say "shessocute."

She said, "What a wasteofmoney."

No, my name is Marissa, I said sweetly.

"Jill needed a doll," said Aunt Alice.

"She can play with the doll you insisted on buying for her sister last year. She doesn't need her own doll, too," said Mother.

"Sally won't share. Besides, she has a fashion doll. I wanted a baby doll," said Jill. "One of my own."

Mother made huffy sounds like an angry train. "When Aunt Alice and I were girls, we didn't have store-bought dolls. We made our own toys," she said.

"Yes. Isn't it nice that we can buy toys for our children now?" said Aunt Alice. "Jill, run along and play while your mother and I talk."

"Chores before play," said Mother.

"Okay," said Jill. "I'll just put Marissa in my room first. Bye, Aunt Alice. Thank you for my doll."

Jill leaned around Aunt Alice to say good-bye to Cousin Ellen. "See you later, alligator."

Cousin Ellen waved good-bye to Jill. She was still hiding. "After a while, crocodile," she whispered.

Jill set me in my doll buggy and pushed me toward the hall. My trunk was tucked under her arm.

"It's your business if you want to spoil Ellen, since she's your own daughter," Mother told Aunt Alice. "However, let me raise my two girls as I see fit."

"A doll's not going to spoil Jill —" said Aunt Alice.

I didn't hear any more.

Jill wheeled me through a hall. Then she took me into a room with two beds.

One bed had a frilly coverlet with yellow rosebuds.

The other bed's coverlet was lime green with big purply flowers. There was an older girl lying on it. Her ponytail was tied with a bow. She was blowing bubbles with her pink gum and popping them. *Smack! Smack!*

The girl didn't even look up. She was busy reading a magazine. It was called *Bobby-soxer Beat*.

Jill pulled me out of the buggy and set me on the yellow rosebud bed. She put my trunk beside me.

"Welcome to your new room, Marissa," she told me.

"Who are you talking to?" the girl on the other bed asked.

"None of your beeswax," said Jill.

The other girl came near. She sat on Jill's bed and stared at me, still popping her gum. *Smack! Smack!* "You're talking to a dumb doll?"

"That's Sally," Jill told me. "She thinks she's cool because she's a teenager. But we don't have to listen to her. She's just my sister."

"Your *big* sister, you mean," Sally reminded her.

Jill nudged Sally. "This is *my* bed. Amscray."

Sally stood up, but she didn't go away. She thumped on my trunk. "Whatcha got in here?"

"I repeat: None of your beeswax," said Jill.

Sally opened the trunk partway and looked in. She made a disappointed, snorty sound. "Baby stuff."

Baby stuff? I thought. I'm the only baby around here. So it was stuff for me. Yippee!

Then Mother came in. She snapped her fingers. "Come on, girls. Time for chores."

Jill and Sally jumped up.

"I'll be right back," Jill promised me. "I'll finish the dusting in record time."

"You'll do it right. Or you'll do it over," Mother said. She sounded strict.

"I know," said Jill.

Jill and Sally left.

Mother came over to me. She picked me up in her big hands.

I tried to look extra-special cute.

She fluffed my gown a little. Then Mother did a surprising thing. She smiled a tiny smile. It was a quick flash, like the store lady's camera. Then she shook her head, and the smile shook off.

"What am I doing?" she muttered. "There's work to be done."

She set me down on the bed and walked out of the room. And I still didn't get to see what was in my trunk.

Wait! What's in the box? I shouted after her.

Pipe down, said a voice. *I'll tell you what's in there.*

I looked up. It was a hard, plastic fashion doll. She

41

stood very prettily on the shelf above Sally's bed. There was a black bow in her stiff blond ponytail.

I can see into the trunk from my shelf. There's a bib, a bottle, diapers, and booties inside it, she told me. *And other baby stuff.*

For me? I asked.

Well, it's not for me, that's for sure, she said.

The fashion doll had a thin waist and little pointy shoes. She wore a white sweater and a wide pink felt skirt. The skirt had a sparkly poodle on it.

I wish I had sparkles, I said.

They're sequins, said the doll.

Is that like penguins? I asked.

No, it's like sequins. This is a grown-up skirt. It's not for baby dolls, said the fashion doll.

I wanted a sparkle poodle, too. More than anything. I forgot my bib, bottle, and diapers. A sparkle poodle was better. Any doll could see that.

How do I grow up? I asked.

The doll laughed. It sounded hollow and plastic. *You don't. You'll always be a baby,* she said.

CHAPTER 11
LOL

♥ ♥ ♥ ♥ ♥

Far Nana yawned. "Okay, that's it for tonight."

Lila moved two gray cats from her lap and set them on the floor. "DSTBC," she said. "Doll Story To Be Continued."

"LOL," said Far Nana.

"What?" asked Lila.

"Nothing," Far Nana said quickly.

"You said LOL. That's computer talk," said Lila.

"It means laughing out loud," said Rose.

"Well, I wonder how I knew that," said Far Nana, sounding puzzled. She hurried into the hallway, jiggling her bead necklaces with one hand.

"I wonder, too," Rose whispered to Lila.

"Yeah," Lila whispered back. "She hates computers."

Far Nana acted like she didn't hear. "Hurry, or you'll be too tired to get up for school tomorrow."

A few minutes later, Rose and Lila were in their bunk beds.

Rose clicked open the locket her parents had given

her before they went to Africa. She kissed the pictures of her mom and dad inside. Then she clicked it shut. She heard Lila do the same with the locket their parents had given her.

Rose lay in her bottom bunk for a few minutes, worrying. What if Bart ratted about seeing her at day care? And about seeing Bunny Boo? Everyone in fourth grade would make fun of her.

I bet I'm the only ten-year-old in the whole town of Oak Hill who still has a baby toy, she thought. How embarrassing.

She bumped the underside of Lila's upper bunk with her foot.

"What?" grumbled Lila.

"Are you asleep?"

"Yes."

"You are not," said Rose.

"I'm talking in my sleep," said Lila.

"Then answer this question in your sleep," said Rose. "How can I make Far Nana believe I'm too sick to go to school tomorrow?"

"Forget it. She won't believe it," said Lila.

"Even if I say I have the mysterious Bunny Boo flu?" joked Rose.

Lila sighed. "Why do you carry Bunny Boo around if you don't want kids to see him?"

"He's good luck," said Rose.

"He didn't bring you luck today. He brought Bart," said Lila.

Rose thought for a minute. "But maybe my luck today would have been even worse without BB," she said. "Did you think of that?"

Lila groaned. "You worry too much."

"I can't help it," said Rose.

"At least think of something more interesting to worry about," said Lila. "Like, what if all the teachers decide to give super-hard pop quizzes tomorrow at school? And we both get Fs. Or what if the lunch ladies make cricket soup, and we have to eat it? Or what if —"

"Okay, okay," said Rose. "What if we go to sleep?"

"Good idea," said Lila. She turned over and pulled up the covers.

Lila is right, thought Rose just before she fell asleep. Carrying BB in her backpack was too risky. She'd take him out in the morning.

CHAPTER 12

Trashland

♥ ♥ ♥ ♥ ♥

I love your new haircut," Rose said to Nadia the next morning on the playground before school. Nadia lived next door to Far Nana, and she was in Rose's class.

"Your braids are gone!" said Lila. She searched Nadia's back like she expected to find the missing braids hiding there.

Nadia smoothed her hair and flipped the short brown ends up. "I got gum stuck in it yesterday. I was going to try to freeze it out with ice. But then I decided to have it cut. I think short hair makes me look older."

"It does," agreed Rose.

Lila nodded. "You look like a sixth-grader."

Nadia smiled and flipped her hair again. "What did you guys do yesterday? I came over, but you weren't home."

"We went to — *ow!*" said Lila.

Rose had nudged Lila hard with her shoulder. She made "are you crazy don't you dare say day care" eyes at her.

"Nothing much," Rose told Nadia. "Far Nana took us out someplace."

"Someplace *doodle dandy*. Wight, *Wose*?" asked a sly voice.

Rose whirled around.

It was Bart and his friend Pete.

Bart had a rubber kick ball. He held it close to his face and rubbed it with one hand, pretending it was a crystal ball.

"I'm Psychic Bart," he said, trying to sound spooky. "My crystal ball sees all, knows all, tells all. I see babies in Wose's past. Wots of them."

Pete pretended to gaze into the kick ball, too. "I see baby games. Wike wing-awound-the-wosie."

"Stop talking baby talk," said Rose.

"Yeah," said Lila. "It's annoying."

"What's the big secret?" Nadia asked Rose and Lila. "Where did you guys go yesterday?"

Bart began to sing:

"Wosie Doodle went to day care,
Wearing stinky diapers.
Stuck a bottle in her mouth
And called it . . ."

Bart looked at Pete for help on the rhyme.

"Windshield wipers?" suggested Pete.

47

Bart rolled his eyes. "Never mind."

Nadia giggled. "You went to day care?" she asked Rose and Lila. "Why?"

"We were going to get baby-sat there," Lila explained. "Only then we helped the day care lady instead."

"Yeah," said Rose. "We were baby-sitting, not being baby-sat."

"What about Bunny Boo?" Bart asked Rose.

Oh, no! thought Rose. She had forgotten to take BB out of her backpack at home that morning.

"What about him?" Lila asked when Rose didn't reply.

Rose held her backpack tighter, protecting BB inside.

Bart's laser eyes saw. "I know a good game. Let's play guess what's in Rose's backpack," he suggested.

"Let's not and say we did," said Rose.

Bart tried to grab her bag just as the bell rang.

"Let's play go to class instead," said Rose.

Bart just grinned his evil grin. Pete copied him.

They all went inside the school building, heading for class.

As she walked down the hall, Rose held her backpack to her chest, with one arm folded around it. With her other hand, she slid BB out. Her heart was thumping. She had to hide him someplace safe before she hung up her backpack in class. If she left him in her bag, Bart would snoop and find him.

But where would BB be safe? Her eyes darted around, looking for a hiding place. Maybe on top of the sixth-graders' lockers?

Bart peeked over her shoulder. "What's in your hand?" he asked.

Rose dropped BB on the hall floor like he was burning her fingers.

"Nothing," she said, quickly scooping him up.

Bart, Pete, Lila, and Nadia gathered around Rose. They stared at BB.

"Looks like a bunny," said Pete.

"It's her Bunny Boo," teased Bart.

"Oh, it's so cute," said Nadia. She petted BB's ears.

Rose shrugged. "My mom and dad gave it to me when I was born. But it's no big deal. I don't like it or anything."

"You don't want it?" asked Bart.

"This ratty old thing?" scoffed Rose. "No way."

"Prove it," said Bart. He got a trash can and held it toward Rose. "Send Bunny Boo to Trashland."

Rose shrugged. "No problem."

Lila gasped. "Don't!" she told Rose.

Too late. Rose dropped her bunny.

He fell down, down, down.

Thump. Bunny Boo hit the bottom of the trash can.

Lila looked down at him and back up at Rose. "You really don't want him?" she asked.

Rose swallowed hard. "Let's go."

On the way to class, Bart sang words to the tune of the Little Rabbit Foo-Foo song:

"Little Bunny Boo Boo
hopped into a trash can.
Kids will throw their trash in
and bop him on the head."

Rose felt terrible. Bart was right. Kids *would* throw trash into the can. And it would land on top of poor BB. She couldn't stand the thought.

She walked a little slower. The minute Bart got ahead of her she would sneak back and rescue BB.

But Bart must have been psychic. He stuck close to her side all the way to class.

During morning math, Rose had a brainstorm. She got a pass for the bathroom. Once she was in the hall, she headed for the trash can. She had to save BB!

Rose looked both ways. No one was around. She stuck a hand into the trash can. Nothing. She turned it upside down.

It was empty!

CHAPTER 13
Baby Face

♥ ♥ ♥ ♥ ♥

When they got home from school, Rose and Lila grabbed granola bars for snacks. Then they went upstairs to the doll hospital.

The baby doll was sitting on a shelf. Its face was covered with white cream.

"What's that goop on Marissa?" Lila asked Far Nana.

Far Nana looked up from the doll bonnet she was mending. "It's acne cream."

Even though she was sad about BB, Rose laughed. "She has pimples?"

"I don't know if it really works on pimples," said Far Nana. "But I do know it will remove ink from doll vinyl. I put it on Marissa last night. On some dolls, it can take a few weeks to work. Fortunately, Marissa's ink stains seem to be soaking off quickly."

Far Nana pulled Marissa off the shelf. She got a cotton pad and wiped some of the cream away.

"How did you figure out that acne cream could clean dolls?" asked Rose.

"I —" Far Nana began. "Uh, I guess I read it somewhere."

Rose squinted at Far Nana. She was keeping secrets.

Far Nana dipped another pad in water and handed it to Rose. "Here. You can help wipe the cream off. Just be careful to keep it away from Marissa's eyes."

Rose forgot about being suspicious. It was fun when Far Nana let them help fix a doll.

Lila looked at Marissa close up as Rose cleaned the doll's face. "It's working!"

"Good thing it wasn't ballpoint-pen ink," said Far Nana. "That can be really hard to remove."

Far Nana picked up a plastic bag. She pulled something yellow and hairy out of it.

"What's that?" asked Lila.

Far Nana shook the hairy thing back and forth, fluffing it out. "A wig for Marissa. Most of her hair was worn off."

She set the wig on a wooden stand shaped like a lightbulb. She began combing the short golden curls. "I was lucky to find this wig. It was made especially for a 1950s baby doll like Marissa."

Rose finished wiping off Marissa's face.

Lila dried it with a soft towel.

Far Nana took the doll and spread glue on the back of its head. Then she carefully positioned the wig on Marissa until it looked just right. She cupped her hands around the wig, pressing it against the doll's head for a few minutes.

Lila noticed two little pieces of black fringe lying on the table. She picked them up. "Fake spiders?" she guessed.

Far Nana chuckled. "They're new doll eyelashes. Good thing the factory that made this baby doll is still in business. I've been able to find a lot of original parts. So Marissa is going to look almost new once the repairs are finished."

Far Nana tugged slightly on the wig and decided it was sticking well enough. She stopped pressing against it and lay Marissa down on her worktable. Carefully, she put a line of glue along the edge of each set of eyelashes. Then she glued one fringe to each of the doll's closed eyelids.

"Can we hear more of the doll story while the glue dries?" asked Lila.

Rose sighed. She couldn't stop thinking about BB.

"Do you want to skip Marissa's story until after dinner?" Far Nana asked her. "You seem a little down in the dumps."

Dumps reminded Rose of trash cans. She groaned.

Lila said, "She's okay. We'll listen." She sat in the big wicker chair. Rose flopped on the window seat and cuddled with the cats.

Far Nana set Marissa in the buggy.

And a moment later the doll's story continued.

CHAPTER 14

Games

Marissa's Story

♥ ♥ ♥ ♥ ♥

I slept until Jill and Sally came back from chores. Jill got right to the important business.

"Let's see what's in your trunk," she suggested.

She sat on the bed and put me in her lap so I could watch. Baby stuff came out of the box. There were more things in there than the poodle-skirt doll had said.

The dangly toy from the store was in there. *Hello, bear! Hello, horse and elephant!* I said.

They were very happy to see me.

Bottles and diapers came out of the box. And more pretty gowns. All for me!

The last thing inside was a pink book, tied with a ribbon. Jill read the words on the front out loud: "Taking Care of Your Baby Doll."

She put it down and looked at all the pretty things on the bed. "What should we do first?" she asked me.

I felt a gentle tug. She was pulling my talking string. *"Let's play,"* I said.

"Good idea!" said Jill. "We'll play House."

House turned out to be a game where I was the baby and Jill was the mama. We were both very good at it. My job was to be cute. And she did all the work. Easy.

First, Jill tied the bib around my neck. Then she took my bottle and left. Was the game over already?

When she came back, the bottle was filled with water.

Jill knelt beside my buggy. "Are you hungry, baby?" she asked.

I don't know, I said.

She put the bottle to my lips. I felt cold, wet drops in my mouth. I didn't know if I liked it or not. Even though Jill couldn't hear me, I cried.

Waa!

I felt the water trickle through me. Soon I felt something cold and wet in my diaper.

Waa! I said again.

"Uh-oh! Baby's got a wet diaper!" said Jill. She sounded happy. Were wet diapers good? They didn't feel good.

"Oh, brother," Sally said from her bed.

Oh, brother, copycatted the poodle-skirt doll.

Jill and I pretended not to hear.

"I'd better change you," Jill said in her busy mama voice.

Jill spread my blankie on her bed. She lay me on it

and took off my wet diaper. She sprinkled snowy-white powder on my bottom.

Then she put a soft, dry diaper on me. It had pink hearts. She pinned it with a bunny pin.

"Now baby's all better," said Jill. She put me on her shoulder and patted my back.

"That doll isn't the only baby around here," said Sally.

Yeah, said the poodle-skirt doll.

"Burp!" Jill said. She pretended I had said it. "That's a good baby."

I practiced drinking and wetting until I got good at it. After a while, I liked drinking. I didn't even mind wetting.

But one time, Jill filled my bottle extra full. It was too much. I felt the drips go to my head. They dripped out of two tiny holes by my eyes. I was a crybaby.

Jill picked me up quick. "Oh! Poor Marissa. Don't cry."

Sally dropped her magazine and came to look at me. "Hot dog!" she said. "Tears are leaking down her face."

"I gave her too much water," Jill said. She sounded worried.

"Don't be silly. She's supposed to be able to cry," said Sally.

Jill rocked me in her arms. "Don't be sad. I'll never make you cry again. I promise."

Sally rolled her eyes and went back to her magazine.

Jill gave me a hug and some kisses.

All my tears dried up.

After that, Jill was careful. She made sure I didn't drink too much. I wasn't a crybaby again.

Jill took me for a ride in the buggy later on. She drove me down the hall. We looked in all the rooms. Except Mother's. My favorite was the shiny black-and-white bathroom.

Then we went outside and parked under a tree. We played a new game called Picnic. It was a game like House, only in the grass.

Neighbors walked by. They all smiled at Jill and me. I smiled back, looking very cute. And everyone loved me, I think.

I saw lots of new faces. But I still liked my mama's face best.

That night, I lay on Jill's pillow, feeling happy.

I didn't have a sparkly poodle skirt. But I had bottles, diapers, and dangly toys. And best of all, I had a mama to keep me safe.

I felt the gentle tug as Jill pulled my string.

When it wound back inside me, I said something new.

"I love you, Ma-ma."

Jill snuggled me close and whispered, "I love you back."

CHAPTER 15

New Faces

Marissa's Story

♥ ♥ ♥ ♥ ♥

As the days went by, I learned new things. I learned that Mother was the biggest grown-up. Sally was the second biggest. And they were both the bosses of Jill and me.

I also learned that Sally was a meanie. Jill said so.

But even though she was a meanie, Sally had friends. When they came, she made us leave our room. I wanted to know what the big girls did in there.

When Mother went to the store one day I finally found out. Sally was supposed to take care of us. Only her friends came over instead.

Jill and I hid in the closet. We played Spy. That's a game where we were very quiet and watched through a crack in the door.

I thought those big girls would do something exciting. They didn't. Unless you think giggling is exciting.

But then the game of Spy got interesting. The girls

61

opened teensy paint boxes. And guess what? They painted their faces!

Jill made a funny squeak when she saw. "They're putting on makeup!"

Sally heard. The closet door opened fast.

"Well, look who's here," said Sally. "It's the baby twins." She pulled us out.

One of her friends tickled my tummy. "Goochie, goochie, goo!" she said.

Jill snatched me away. "Leave her alone."

Sally's friends all laughed.

"Don't go ape," one of them teased.

"When Mother comes home, I'm telling," Jill warned Sally. "You're not supposed to wear mascara or lipstick until you're sixteen!"

"You're such a square," said Sally. She squinted her eyes. They had thick, extra-long makeup lashes.

"Beat it, babies," she said. She pushed us into the hall and shut the door behind us.

"She thinks she's so grown-up," Jill grumped. "I'll show her. I'm just as grown-up as she is."

Jill wheeled me into Mother's room. I had never seen it before. It had a mirror with lightbulbs along the edges. I got to sit on the table in front of it. There were little boxes around me. They had surprises inside.

Jill opened a long round one. Out came a red stick.

She smeared the red stick on her lips. Now they looked extra big.

She opened a flat box. She dusted blue stuff on her eyelids. They looked sparkly when she blinked.

Another box had pink inside. She smeared pink on her cheeks.

"How do I look?" she asked me.

Pretty, I told her.

"What's going on here?" someone boomed from nearby.

Jill sucked in a loud breath. She turned around.

Mother's home! I said.

Mother stood behind us in the doorway. I could see her in the mirror. She made her upside-down smile.

"What are you doing with my makeup?" she asked.

"Just pretending," Jill said in a small voice.

Mother was in a mad huff. "Lipstick and eye shadow are expensive. They're not for children." She grabbed the blue sparkle-powder away from Jill and clicked its case shut. She closed the lipstick.

Sally came in. She had washed her paint off. Her eyes got big when she saw Jill's pretty new face. "You're in for it now," she said.

"That's enough, young lady," Mother told Sally. She pointed to the door. "Go to your room."

"I didn't do anything!" said Sally. But she went.

"I'm sorry," Jill said to Mother. "But I wasn't the only one trying on makeup —"

"Don't try to shift the blame," said Mother. She wiped the pretty paint from Jill's face. Then she saw me and her eyes got extra mad. She looked from me to Jill.

"If you're grown-up enough to wear makeup, you must be too old for dolls," she said. She stepped toward me.

Jill rushed to get between me and Mother. "No! I'm not too old for Marissa!"

Mother didn't listen. "Cousin Ellen is just the right age for a baby doll. She'll get a lot of pleasure playing with this one now that you've outgrown it."

Mother came closer.

Jill reached her arms behind and squeezed me to her back. "No, Mother. Please! Don't take Marissa."

But Mother's big hands took me away from Jill's little ones.

"Come on," said Mother.

We went outside to the car. I sat in the backseat. Mother and Jill sat in the front.

Hey! It's lonely back here! Where are we going, anyway? I asked.

Jill peeked into the back at me. Her upside-down smile made me scared. I hushed up.

We rode away to a different house. Inside were Aunt Alice and Cousin Ellen.

Mother put me in Cousin Ellen's hands. Icky sticky.

Aunt Alice looked unhappy to see me there.

Jill stared sadly at me.

"Good-bye, Marissa," she whispered. "I love you."

Don't leave me, Ma–ma, I begged.

Mother put a hand on Jill's shoulder. "Let's go."

They went. And they left me behind.

CHAPTER 16
New Friends
Marissa's Story

Cousin Ellen grinned at me. "Now I'm your mama."

Nope, I said.

She took me to her room anyway.

"Talk, dolly!" Cousin Ellen pulled my string. She did it again and again and again. I talked until I got a horsey throat.

After a while, she tossed me in her toy box and left.

I remember you, said a growly voice.

It was Mr. Fuzzy! He was in the toy box, too. Only he wasn't so fuzzy anymore. He had bare patches.

What happened to your fur? I asked.

A raggedy voice began to sing:

Fuzzy Wuzzy was a bear,
Fuzzy Wuzzy had no hair,
Fuzzy Wuzzy wasn't fuzzy, was he?

It was a rag doll with one button eye. Next to her was a toy puppy without a tail. And a fairy princess doll with a broken wand.

Stop being cruel, the fairy princess told the rag doll. I liked her tiny sweet voice.

Cousin Ellen pulled my fur out, Mr. Fuzzy told me. *She breaks all her toys.*

She plays ruff! Ruff! barked the puppy.

Is she a meanie? I asked.

She's just too young to know better, said the fairy princess.

Are you her new doll? the puppy asked me.

No, I said.

Then what are you doing here? asked Mr. Fuzzy.

Mother gave me to Cousin Ellen. My mama, Jill, couldn't stop her.

I guess your mama didn't love you, said the rag doll.

She does too love me, I said.

Then why did she give you away? asked the rag doll.

She didn't. Mother did.

The other toys didn't understand.

Never mind, I said. I was too tired to explain.

Everyone else fell asleep after a while. But I stayed awake in the toy box all that night, worrying.

I tried to be brave.

But it wasn't easy.

CHAPTER 17

Beautiful

Marissa's Story

♥ ♥ ♥ ♥ ♥

The next day, Cousin Ellen played a game called Art. For Art, she got paper and markers. She drew a picture of black flowers and blue trees and a purple house. Then she drew a picture of me. She drew my eyes yellow and my cheeks purple.

That does not look like me, I said. But she did not listen.

Next we played a new game. It was called Beauty Shop.

Cousin Ellen put me in a chair.

"Now, Mrs. Baby Dolly, I'll make you look grown-up for the party," she told me.

What party? I asked.

She didn't answer. She was too busy with scissors. *Snip! Snip! Snip!* I saw a pile of hair on the floor. My hair.

Then she got her markers. The purple marker came closer and closer. It squished against my cheek. She cir-

cled it around and around. Cousin Ellen was drawing on my face!

"There!" she said. "Now you look like my picture. You are bee-yoo-tee-ful!"

I waited for the party. But it never came. I went back into the toy box.

The rag doll laughed when she saw me. *What's on your face?*

Don't you know anything? I asked her. *It's called makeup. Only grown-ups get to wear it.*

The other dolls looked impressed.

You're not a grown-up, said the rag doll.

She looks older to me, said the fairy princess.

I smiled at her. *Thank you.*

I stayed in the toy box for a long time after that. I missed Jill over and over.

One day, Cousin Ellen decided to play Picnic.

Don't worry. Picnic is a fun game, I told the other toys.

Cousin Ellen spread a blanket on the grass outside. She took Mr. Fuzzy, the fairy princess, and me out there.

"Now, let's all have tea," she told us.

We each got a china cup. Mine was cracked. And empty.

We each got a sugar cookie. Cousin Ellen ate them all for us, very helpfully.

After a while, Aunt Alice called us to come in.

Cousin Ellen wrapped the blanket around herself like a cape. She grabbed Mr. Fuzzy in one hand and the fairy princess in the other. "I'm Super Ellen!" she shouted. Her cape fluttered out behind her as she ran inside.

What about me? I yelled.

But she did not come back.

Nighttime came. It was spooky. I lay outside, all by myself.

Babies can't stay outside, I said, like a scaredy-cat.

But I had no choice. Cousin Ellen had forgotten me.

Days and days went by.

Butterflies took naps on my nose.

Ladybugs made their home in my gown.

Robins pulled hair from my head to make nests.

The grass grew tall around me.

One morning, I heard a loud rumbly noise. I saw a man. He was pushing a grass-gobbling machine! It came nearer. Was it going to gobble me, too?

Suddenly, the gobbling stopped.

The man bent down and stared at me. His shirt pocket had the name LARRY'S LAWN MOWING SERVICE.

"Kids and their toys," he grumbled. He picked me up and tossed me into the flower garden.

The flowers were kind and pretty. Their names were Lily and Snapdragon. They let me smell their perfume each morning. And if the sun got too hot, they gave me shade. Even though I was still outside, things were better.

Until the day the wind came.

The trees were the first to notice it. They leaned over to warn us. *Storm's brewing,* they said.

The flowers looked up.

Thunder's coming, said Snapdragon.

Oh, dear, said Lily. *Lightning, too, from the looks of things.*

I looked up.

Mad clouds blew overhead. Sparks shot across the sky, making thunder sounds.

I'm scared, I said.

The flowers bent low, protecting me.

Water began to fall from the sky. It went drip, drip, drip into the tiny hole in my lips. It filled me up full.

Tears rained down my cheeks.

I was crying.

CHAPTER 18
Don't Ask

♥ ♥ ♥ ♥ ♥

The doll hospital grew silent.

"Is that it?" asked Lila. She was afraid to hear the answer. "Did Marissa lie in that yard forever?"

"That can't be it," said Rose. "Jill has to come and get her. Because she has her now. Right?"

"Marissa's story isn't finished," said Far Nana. She got up and stretched. "But we have to stop for the night."

"Don't say we're stopping because we have to get up for school," said Rose. "You always say that."

"Because it's true," said Far Nana. "But this time, I'm the one who has to get up tomorrow. I've got plans again."

Lila opened her mouth. "Where are you —?"

Rose elbowed her. "Don't ask," she whispered.

Far Nana didn't hear. She was already out in the hall. "Come on. Let's go get dinner. Then homework and bed."

CHAPTER 19
Baby Toys

♥ ♥ ♥ ♥ ♥

I'm mad at you," Lila told Rose after school the next day. She and Rose were walking across the playground, toward home.

"What did I do?" Rose asked in surprise.

"You threw Bunny Boo away. Don't you even miss him?" asked Lila.

"Yes! For your information, I went back to try to find him in the trash," said Rose. She kicked a stone out of her path. "But he was gone."

"I know he was," said Lila. "Because I rescued him. Here." She slapped something fuzzy into Rose's hand.

It was BB!

"*You* were the bunny-napper?" asked Rose.

Lila nodded. "I hung around the trash can until Bart left. Then I saved Bunny Boo for you."

Rose rubbed BB's soft fur against her chin. "Why didn't you give him back to me sooner?"

"I told you. I was mad at you," said Lila. "Mom and Dad gave you Bunny Boo. Doesn't he matter to you?"

"Yeah," said Rose. "He does. But what was I supposed to do when Bart —"

Lila nudged Rose. "Look out," she warned.

Up ahead, Rose saw Nadia, Bart, and some other kids. Before she had a chance to hide her toy, Nadia and Bart walked over.

Bart laughed when he saw Bunny Boo. "You got Dumpster-bunny out of the trash? Gross!"

Rose shrugged, turning pink.

Nadia petted BB. "I think he's cute."

"You don't think he's too babyish?" asked Rose.

Nadia shook her head no. "I have a little stuffed pony from when I was a baby. I named him Apple-loosa. My mom said I used to take him everywhere I went."

"That's so lame," said Bart.

Nadia frowned at him. "It is not. My mom says I'll be glad I have Apple-loosa when I grow up. She still has her favorite toy from when she was a baby. Don't you have any of your baby toys left?"

"Yeah, right," said Bart. "Boys don't have baby toys."

Just then, something grabbed Rose around the knees. She looked down.

It was Beth. Bryan was with her.

Rose smiled. "Hi, boa-girl."

"Hi, Beth," said Lila. "Hi, Bryan."

Bryan giggled when he saw what Rose was holding. "Bunny Boo!"

Rose looked over and saw Beth, Bryan, and Bart's mom standing by the blue car. She was picking up Bart after school.

"Come on, kids!" she called.

Suddenly, Rose had an idea. "Hey, Bryan, does Bart still have any stuff from when he was a baby?" she asked quickly.

"No!" Bart butted in.

Too late.

Bryan popped his thumb out of his mouth and said, "Blankie."

Rose grinned. "Bart has a blankie?"

Bryan nodded.

"I do not," said Bart. He pulled Bryan toward the car.

"Do, too," said Bryan.

"Oh, how cute! Bart has a blankie," teased Nadia.

Rose and Lila giggled.

Bart frowned. "He doesn't know what he's talking about," he called back to them. "He's just three."

"I'm fwee!" Beth announced.

"C'mon, Beth!" Bart's mom called.

Beth let go of Rose and ran for the car.

"Don't be embarrassed about your baby blanket," the girls heard Bart's mom tell him. "Lots of kids have keepsakes from when they were little."

Rose, Lila, and Nadia laughed as the blue car drove

away. Rose put BB in her backpack. Then, together, the three girls walked toward home.

"I can't believe it," said Rose. "Bart has a baby blanket!"

"I bet he used to drool on it," said Nadia.

"Probably still does," said Lila.

They all laughed again.

When they got to Far Nana's, Rose and Lila waved good-bye to Nadia. Then they hurried inside and upstairs.

They dropped their backpacks in the hall and ran into the witch's hat. They sat down fast.

Far Nana was knitting. She was fixing a hole in Marissa's bootie.

"Let's finish," Rose and Lila told her.

Far Nana knew what they meant. She nodded and set Marissa in the buggy.

Soon afterward, the baby doll's story continued.

CHAPTER 20
Tears
Marissa's Story

♥ ♥ ♥ ♥ ♥

I waited and waited and waited.

And one day,

Mama

finally

came.

I saw her through a window. She was inside Aunt Alice's house. She had on a grumpy face.

I saw Cousin Ellen in there, too. She pointed out the window at the backyard.

Jill came outside. Her head turned this way and that, very fast. Her two ponytails slapped back and forth. She was looking for something.

Aunt Alice and Cousin Ellen came outside, too.

"You left Marissa in the yard?" Aunt Alice asked Cousin Ellen.

"We played Picnic. And I forgot her," said Cousin Ellen.

"I'm so sorry," Aunt Alice told Jill. "I didn't know."

"It's okay," Jill said, in a hurry-up voice. "Just help us find her, Cousin Ellen."

Cousin Ellen looked around in the grass. "We played Picnic right here. But I don't see her now."

The three of them searched the yard. No one saw me in the flower garden.

I'm over here, Ma-ma! I called.

Suddenly, Jill turned toward me. The flowers swayed away, uncovering me.

"There she is!" Jill shouted.

She rushed across the yard and knelt on the grass beside me. She picked me up with her small gentle hands.

Jill must have drunk too much water. Because she was the crybaby this time. I didn't even know she could make tears like me!

"Oh, my poor baby," Jill said, rocking me from side to side.

Aunt Alice and Cousin Ellen hurried over.

Jill stuck me out so they could see. "Look what happened to Marissa!"

"I'm sorry," said Cousin Ellen.

"I don't blame you," said Jill.

Me, either, I said.

"You're little," Jill went on. "You didn't know any better. I blame Mother for this. It's all her fault!"

Jill took me and ran toward the house.

Bye-bye, flowers, I told my pretty friends. *I'm going home!*

But instead of taking me home, Jill took me into Cousin Ellen's bedroom. She slammed the door shut and sat on the bed.

She looked at me sadly. She touched my purple cheeks. She patted my chopped-short curls.

I got makeup! I said proudly.

"You're still pretty, anyway," she told me.

I know! I said.

A few minutes later, Aunt Alice knocked and came in.

"I called your mother. She'll be here to pick you up soon," she said.

Uh-oh! Mother's coming, I said.

"And I told her what happened to Marissa," Aunt Alice added.

"Good. Because I'm never, ever going to speak to her again," said Jill.

"Don't say that," said Aunt Alice. Her wide skirt swished as she sat beside us.

"But Mother made me break my promise. I told that lady at the doll store I'd take care of Marissa forever and ever! Remember?" Jill said.

"Your mother didn't mean to hurt you," said Aunt Alice. "She just doesn't understand dolls. We never had them when we were growing up."

"But *you* understand," said Jill.

Aunt Alice made a puff-breath sound. "Growing up was harder for your mother than it was for me. Our mom — your grandmother — died when I was six. Your mother was just ten."

"I know," said Jill.

"But what you don't know," Aunt Alice continued, "is that your mother had to become a grown-up at ten years old."

"Why?" asked Jill.

"After our mom died, our dad still had to go to work every day. So your mother did all the chores when we got home from school. She took care of me and the house."

"That sounds hard," said Jill.

Aunt Alice nodded. "She had to act like a grown-up. She didn't have time for playing. If she played hop-scotch, dinner didn't get cooked. If she played a board game, the clothes didn't get washed."

"What if she played dolls?" Jill asked softly.

"There wasn't money for dolls," said Aunt Alice. "But if there had been, she wouldn't have had time to play with them."

How sad! I said.

"That's sad," said Jill.

Aunt Alice smiled. "We were lucky in some ways. Your mother and I had a home. And our dad loved us. So it wasn't really that bad. But because she didn't get to play much as a child, your mother doesn't understand how important Marissa is to you."

Someone knocked on the door. Mother came in.

She looked at Jill. She looked at me. Then she said, "Come on, now. Let's go home."

CHAPTER 21

Love

Marissa's Story

♥ ♥ ♥ ♥ ♥

The car was quiet inside as Mother drove us home. This time, I got to sit in the front seat, on Jill's lap.

I wanted to hurry up. What if Mother took me away from Jill again?

But Mother drove us home, all safe.

Jill pulled the car door handle. The door clicked open.

Then Mother put a hand on Jill's arm. "Wait."

Oh, no! Was Mother going to take me back to Cousin Ellen's?

Jill turned her head a little to peek at Mother.

I looked out the car window. At the end of the sidewalk was home. I wanted to go inside right then.

But Mother began talking.

"I'm sorry I made you give Marissa away," she told Jill. "I was wrong. Sometimes I forget you're only eight."

"So I can keep her?" asked Jill. "I can keep Marissa?"

Mother smiled a tiny smile. "You can keep her."

Yippee! I said.

Jill gave her mother a hug. "Thank you!"

Mother hugged back. I got squished in between. It felt happy.

"Let's go inside," said Mother.

Hooray! We were home for good.

Here I come, dangle toys! Hello, buggy! Hello, poodle-skirt doll! I shouted. *I'm back home forever and ever!*

Everyone was glad to see me. They asked me how my face and hair got so different.

I told them all about Beauty Shop. And guess what? They didn't even know that game!

They told me something, too. The picture of Jill and me from the doll store had come in the mail. It was sitting right there on Jill's nightstand, looking important.

I didn't have much time to chat, though. Because Jill started taking care of me right away. She gave me a warm bath in my favorite room of all — the bathroom! She gave my gown and bonnet a bath, too.

When I got dry, my clothes were still wet. So Jill dressed me in a new dress. I got wrapped in my blankie. I was snuggly safe.

I felt a gentle tug at the back of my neck. Jill had pulled my talking string. She smiled at me, waiting.

The string wound back inside me. I tried to speak.

But no words came out!

Jill got an upside-down smile. She pulled my talking string again.

This time, I made a *grrr-thnk* sound. But I didn't talk!

Jill looked at me sadly. She rubbed her polka-dot cheek against my scribbly one.

"It's okay," she whispered. "I love you, anyway. Even if you can't talk anymore."

I sat silent and still.

I loved my mama. More than ever. But I couldn't tell her. Not that day. Not the next or the next.

I never talked again.

CHAPTER 22
Surfing

♥ ♥ ♥ ♥ ♥

Rose groaned. "That ending stinks."

"It's not going to stink when Far Nana makes Marissa talk again," said Lila. "Then it will be a good-smelling kind of story ending."

"I was just getting to that," said Far Nana.

She picked up a small metal box from her worktable.

"What's that?" asked Lila.

"It's a voice box for Marissa," said Far Nana. "It came in the mail today."

"Where did you buy it?" asked Rose.

Far Nana was quiet for a second. Then she set the voice box down. She jiggled her bead necklaces, then sighed, then jiggled again. She was nervous.

"If you must know, I used the computer at the library to order it," she told them. "From a Web site. That's how I found the acne cream and Marissa's wig, too."

"You used a computer?" Rose asked in an amazed voice.

Far Nana nodded. "I've been taking a computer class

two days a week. That's where I was when I left you at Ms. Jill's."

"Cool!" said Lila.

"Cool?" Far Nana echoed in surprise. "I thought you might tease me because I was so against computers to begin with. I hate to eat crow."

Rose and Lila looked at each other.

"We won't make you eat crow," said Rose.

"Whatever that means," said Lila.

"Why did you change your mind about computers?" asked Rose.

"Another doll doctor told me the Internet is a great resource for doll supplies. So I decided to take a computer class and see what computers are all about," Far Nana explained. "I was afraid I might be the oldest one in the class. But I'm not. There's a ninety-year-old man in it, too!"

"No way," said Lila.

"Way," said Far Nana.

"This is so great. Now you can make a Web site for your doll hospital!" said Rose.

Far Nana looked excited. "I'm not that advanced yet. I have a lot to learn. But I'm catching on."

"We'd better buy you a tiny surfboard," said Lila.

Rose and Far Nana gave her puzzled looks.

"So you can surf the Internet!" said Lila.

Rose grinned. "And we'll have to buy you a space suit. For cyberspace."

Rose and Lila smacked a high five with each other.

"LOL," said Far Nana.

"Does this mean you're going to buy a computer?" asked Rose.

"Ohpleaseohpleaseohplease?" begged Lila.

"And don't forget a TV," added Rose.

"Yeah! We need one of those, too," said Lila.

"We'll see," said Far Nana.

CHAPTER 23
Voice Box

♥ ♥ ♥ ♥ ♥

Far Nana let Rose and Lila undress Marissa so she could finish repairing her. Then she lay the doll facedown on her worktable. She picked up a tool with a sharp blade and cut a straight line down Marissa's back.

Rose and Lila gasped.

"Relax. She doesn't feel a thing," said Far Nana. "Her drinking tube is clogged. I've got to clean it out. And this is the only way to reach it."

She stuck a cotton swab into the slit in the doll's vinyl body. She moved it up and down in Marissa's drinking tube. Then she pulled the swab out.

Next, she tugged a rusty metal box out of the doll.

"It's her old voice box," said Far Nana. "The rain probably rusted it when Marissa got caught in that storm."

"So that's why she couldn't speak?" asked Rose.

Far Nana nodded. She poked the new voice box in through the doll's back. It slid into place.

"This isn't the same kind of voice box. I couldn't

match Marissa's original one exactly. But this should do the trick," she said. She tinkered with it a while, using different tools.

"There," she said finally. She set Marissa upright. "Are you ready to talk?" she asked her.

Lila put her finger through the loop at the end of the pull string that made the doll talk. "Can I do it?"

Far Nana nodded.

Lila pulled the string carefully. Then she let go. The string slid slowly back into the doll.

They all watched Marissa closely. But nothing happened.

Far Nana frowned. "Try it again."

Lila pulled the string. "Simon says: Talk."

She let go. Marissa still didn't speak.

"What's wrong?" asked Rose.

"Maybe she has amnesia," said Lila.

"No. That's when you can't remember stuff," said Rose. "Laryngitis is when you can't talk."

"I don't get it," Far Nana said. "This should work." She lay Marissa down on her worktable again. She fiddled with the voice box some more.

She set the doll upright and pulled the doll's talking string out as far as it would go. She let loose and the pull string wound back inside.

But Marissa just stared at them with silent eyes.

CHAPTER 24
Silence

♥ ♥ ♥ ♥ ♥

Marissa still wasn't talking by the next afternoon when Ms. Jill arrived to pick her up.

Far Nana had sealed her body closed anyway and dressed her again.

"Oh, she looks great!" Ms. Jill said when she saw her doll. She smiled, but she had tears in her eyes.

"Only there's still one teeny, tiny problem," said Lila, trying to warn her.

"Whatever it is, I don't care. I'm just glad to have her back and looking so well," said Ms. Jill.

"You might be a little disappointed," said Rose.

"I did my best, but . . ." Far Nana began at the same time.

Before they could explain, Ms. Jill pulled Marissa's talking string.

Far Nana, Rose, and Lila watched the doll, expecting silence.

Ms. Jill gazed happily at her doll, waiting. Marissa's blue eyes stared back at her.

The string slid slowly, slowly back inside the doll. And then — something amazing happened.

Marissa spoke! Her single word floated softly in the room, wrapping itself around them.

"*Ma-ma.*"

Questions and Answers About the 1950s

How were the 1950s different from today?
The way Americans lived in the 1950s was similar to the way we live today. But there were some differences.

Back then, people dressed differently than we do now.

And there weren't as many entertainment choices.

Workers earned less money at their jobs. But groceries, clothing, homes, cars, and almost everything else cost less then than they do today.

Most men had jobs outside the home in the 1950s. But married women were usually homemakers and stay-at-home moms. Not many had jobs outside the home.

What did people wear in the 1950s?
In the 1950s, girls were not allowed to wear pants or shorts to school. They wore skirts or dresses, often with stiff petticoats underneath. Dresses or skirts were worn on public outings — even to restaurants or movies! The only time most girls and women wore pants or shorts was at home.

White socks called bobby socks were popular with girls, especially teenagers. Girls and women sometimes wore white gloves when they got really dressed up. Shoes called penny loafers were popular. They had a slot on top where a penny was inserted.

Many women wore their hair short and styled stiffly with hair spray. Some men used oil or tonic to make their hair stay the way they combed it.

What did kids do for fun in the 1950s?

Most kids in the 1950s had fewer toys than kids do today. Some toys that were popular back then are still popular today. Those include the Slinky and the Hula Hoop.

Television got its start in the 1920s and 1930s. But by 1950, only 9 percent of American homes had a TV. Just ten years later, in 1960, almost 88 percent of American homes had a TV. Everyone in the family had to watch the same show, because usually there was only one TV in the house.

Most TV shows in the 1950s were filmed in black and white. Popular shows included *The Lone Ranger*, *Lassie*, and *Leave It to Beaver*.

In the 1950s, there were no home computers, computer games, or shopping malls. There weren't any DVDs, CDs, or cell phones. Kids listened to music on transistor radios. If they were lucky, they might own a small record player.

Drive-in movies were popular. At this kind of theater, families sat in their cars to watch movies on a big outdoor screen. Most families had only one car.

In the 1950s, 3-D movies were developed. *Creature from the Black Lagoon* and *It Came from Outer Space* were two hit 3-D movies.

Words and Terms
Used in the 1950s

Beat It! or Get Lost!   Leave! or Go away!

beehive   a woman's tall, hair-sprayed hairdo

bobby-soxer   girl who wore a wide skirt, a sweater, and thick white ankle socks

cat   a cool person

Cool it!   Relax!

cruisin' for a bruisin'   looking for trouble

daddy-o   a cool guy

DDT   Drop Dead Twice (something people said to be mean)

dig   to like something

flip   to get excited

flip out   to get angry

a gas   something exciting or fun

go ape   get angry or excited

goof   a person who makes mistakes

grody   messy

hipster   a cool person

Hot dog!   Oh, good! or That's interesting!

idiot box   TV

Later, gator!   I'll see you later!

Like, wow!   That's great!

nowheresville   a boring place

on cloud nine   very happy

pad   home

party pooper   a person who's no fun

pile up some z's   sleep

Razz my berries   Tell me something exciting

sing   tattle

sock hop   a dance party

split   leave

square   a boring person who follows the rules

threads   clothes

a Washington   a dollar

wet rag   a boring person

whirlybird   helicopter

Watch for the next book in the
Doll Hospital™ series,

Danielle's Dollhouse Wish,

coming soon.

P retend you're Far Nana," Lila told Rose as they walked home from school.

"Why?" asked Rose.

"I have to introduce her to my teacher on Parents' Night," said Lila. "We're supposed to practice."

Rose wondered if Lila felt sad that their parents couldn't come for Parents' Night. She didn't ask because she didn't want to make Lila sad, too. If she wasn't already.

"Okay," she said. Rose jiggled her heart-shaped locket, since Far Nana always jiggled her bead necklaces. She made pretend eyeglasses with her thumbs and first fingers. She held them up to her eyes and looked over the tops of them at Lila.

"Have you done your homework?" she asked in a bossy, grown-up voice.

Lila didn't answer. She looked to the side and began speaking to the air. "May I present my grandmother?"

105

Rose looked around. "Who are you talking to?" she asked.

"My teacher. I'm pretending that I'm introducing Far Nana to him," explained Lila.

"Oh." Rose switched back to her Far Nana voice. "How do you do," she told the imaginary teacher.

"Far Nana, may I present my teacher, Mr. Yi," Lila said.

Rose dropped her finger-glasses. "You've got it down," she said, speaking in her normal voice again. "You can stop practicing."

"I know. It's just that all the kids are going to do it the same way. I wish I could make my introduction more special. But — Hey, what's that?" asked Lila, pointing ahead.

Rose looked.

A large wooden crate sat on Far Nana's porch. A delivery truck was parked in the street by the curb.

"Maybe it's a present from Mom and Dad!" Lila took off running.

Rose followed, her long blond hair flying behind her. The key-chain charms dangling from her backpack tapped together with each step.

They ran past three driveways to Far Nana's house and then up the front steps. Rose and Lila walked around the crate on the porch, studying it from all sides.

"I bet it's a computer!" guessed Lila.

Rose shook her head. "No. It's too tall."

"A refrigerator?" asked Lila.

"Too short," said Rose. She read the mailing label. "It's from the Dollhouse Museum of Washington, D.C."

"A dollhouse! Cool!" said Lila. Her beagle backpack bounced against her back as she hopped with excitement.

Far Nana came out of the house. "Careful, girls."

A deliveryman with a wheeled dolly cart stepped out the front door behind her. He nodded hello to Rose and Lila. Then he expertly scooted the crate on to the dolly and rolled it inside the house.

The dolly bumped upstairs behind him, one stair at a time. Far Nana guided him into a turreted room on the third floor. The man went in and set the crate on the floor.

"I need to get something to open the crate. Be right back," Far Nana said.

"Okay." The man didn't really look like he was listening. He looked surprised as he stared around the inside of the room.

"This is a doll hospital," Rose told him.

"Our grandmother is a doll doctor," Lila added.

The deliveryman patted the tall crate, smiling. "This must be a mighty big doll."

He wheeled his dolly cart out the door before the girls could explain.

When Far Nana came back, she held a metal crowbar in one hand.

"Is there really a dollhouse in this box?" asked Rose.

"Should be. That's what I was expecting," said Far Nana.

"Can we open it?" asked Lila.

"That's the plan," said Far Nana. She wedged the crowbar under the crate's lid and pulled. When the lid popped up, she slid it off.

Far Nana and Rose looked in the top of the crate.

"What do you see?" asked Lila. She stretched on tiptoe but was too short to see inside.

"Just plastic wrap so far," said Rose.

Far Nana now pried boards away from the sides of the crate. She handed each board that she pulled off to Rose and Lila. "Would you carry them out to the back porch?" she asked. "Stack them carefully. I'll need them to recrate the dollhouse when it's time to return it to the museum."

Rose and Lila went up and down the stairs several times, taking pieces of the crate outside.

Soon, the dollhouse was uncrated. Then all three helped peel off the protective plastic wrapped around it.

When the last of it came off, they stared.

The painted wooden dollhouse was four stories tall. Wooden shutters framed the dainty lace curtains hanging at each window. A pot of pink flowers sat on either side of the double front doors.

"It's so cool!" said Lila. "This is one of the best things you've ever gotten to fix." She walked around the house on her knees, looking it over.

"It is lovely, isn't it?" their grandmother agreed.

"What's wrong with it anyway?" asked Rose.

"It needs work here and there. That's why the museum sent it to me," said Far Nana.

The girls took a closer look and began to notice the damage.

Some of the roof's shingles were missing. One corner of the house was dented, as though it had been bumped. The railing on the front steps was broken and the paint was chipped in places.

Rose pointed to a sign over the front door that read LA MAISON DE POUPÉE. "What does that say?"

Lila read it aloud. "Lay Mason dee Poopy."

Far Nana laughed. "It's pronounced, Lah May-ZOHN duh PooPAY. That's French for The House of Dolls. Or Dollhouse."

"So it's from France?" asked Rose.

"The letter I got from the museum last week said the house was made in Paris around 1890," said Far Nana.

Far Nana cleared space on her worktable, and the three of them lifted the dollhouse onto the table. It took up a lot of room.

Rose and Lila looked through its small windows.

"It's too dark in there," complained Lila. "I can't see anything."

"How does it open?" asked Rose.

"The front panel comes off," said Far Nana.

She poked a screwdriver in the slit where the front of the house fit against the side. She gently wiggled the tool back and forth. Soon, the front panel pushed forward. She pulled it off and set it on the floor, leaning it against one leg of her worktable.

Lila and Rose looked in the dollhouse's rooms. Some were as big as shoe boxes. Others were as small as juice boxes. And some were sized in between.

Most of the walls were covered with wallpaper, but some were painted. There were fireplaces in several rooms. A spiral staircase wound up through the middle of the house.

"There are thirteen rooms," Lila counted.

"There are three more in the attic," said Far Nana. She lifted the roof off to show them the little rooms underneath it.

"Cool," said Lila.

"Why are they all empty?" asked Rose.

Lila frowned. "Yeah. Where's all the stuff that goes inside? Like beds and tables and chairs."

"The furniture is in the other crate," said Far Nana. She picked up her notebook and began writing.

"What other crate?" asked Rose.

Without looking up from her notes, Far Nana mumbled, "The one behind the door." The girls could tell she was already thinking of ways to fix the dollhouse.

Rose and Lila rushed to look. Behind the door of the witch's hat, they found a TV-sized crate.

"How did we miss seeing this?" asked Lila.

"The delivery guy must've brought it in before we got here," said Rose.

Lila knelt down and tugged at the top of the crate. "It won't open."

"We'd better ask first, anyway," said Rose.

She turned to their grandmother. "Far Nana?"

"Hmmm?"

"Can we look at the furniture?"

"That would be a big help. All those little pieces take a long time to unwrap," said Far Nana. She used the crowbar to open the smaller crate for them.

"Yay!" Lila said, bouncing happily when she saw the little packages inside.

"Just be careful!" said Far Nana. "And put everything on the shelves I've emptied on the wall as you unpack."

"We will," Rose and Lila said at the same time.

Before Rose and Lila could begin unwrapping, Far Nana's three gray cats began sniffing around the crate.

"Shoo," said Rose.

The cats didn't shoo.

"You'd better put them outside for a while," said Far Nana.

"Good idea," said Lila. "They might chew on the furniture."

Rose carried two cats downstairs and Lila carried one. When Lila opened the front door, the three cats scooted out to play in the yard.

Once they were back upstairs, Rose looked around for Far Nana's fourth cat, the only black one. "Where's Ringo?" she asked.

"I don't know," said Lila. "Look at this! A little piano and a cracked mirror." She had already unwrapped two pieces of doll-sized furniture.

Rose sat next to the crate and pulled one of the plastic-wrapped things from inside it.

They both unwrapped chairs, tables, pictures, and dishes, showing each other what they discovered.

"Tiny books!" said Rose. "They really open! And they even have words inside."

"A canopy bed!" said Lila.

Rose looked over. "Ooh! I love those."

Lila wiggled one of the bed's legs. "It's a little bit broken."

"So is this bathtub," said Rose. "It's chipped."

"But most of the stuff isn't broken. Just dirty," said Lila.

At the bottom of the crate, they found a red velvet box. A gold rope with tassels on each end was tied around it.

Rose untied the rope and opened the box. The

things inside were wrapped in tissue paper. They were the size of saltshakers.

Lila scooted over to look. "What are they?"

"Special furniture, I guess," said Rose.

They each lifted one out and unwrapped it.

Rose finished first. "A little girl doll!" It was about four inches long. She held it up so Lila could see.

The girl doll wore a long blue dress, black stockings, and blue slippers. Her curly blond hair was covered with a straw bonnet decorated with flowers.

"Mine's a bigger girl," said Lila. She showed Rose the doll she'd unwrapped. It was about six inches long and wore a peach silk dress edged with lace. Its hair was twisted into a bun held in place with a jeweled comb.

"Maybe it's the mother doll," said Rose.

"Rose! Lila!" called Far Nana. "Come look!"

The girls stood and went over to Far Nana's worktable. Now the dollhouse was even more beautiful. Its candles, chandeliers, and fireplaces glowed with dim, golden light.

"The house is wired for electricity," said Far Nana. "Isn't it pretty?"

"It's even cooler than before," said Lila.

Photo by George Hallowell

Joan Holub

About the Author

When Joan Holub was a girl, her best friend, Ann, lived right down the street. Ann had lots of toys. But she had one special doll that Joan loved best — a beautiful ballerina. The doll had lace-up shoes and a frilly satin tutu. Her body was jointed and bendable.

After a few years, Joan's family moved away. Ann gave the doll to Joan as a going-away present. Joan named the doll Annie, after her friend. She made lots of clothes for Annie, using her mother's sewing machine.

Joan played with Annie so much that she wore her out. Annie's arms and legs came apart. She needed help! So Joan and her mother took Annie to a doll hospital. There, Annie's arms and legs were put back together. She even got a new wig.

Annie and some of her doll friends still live in Washington State with Joan, her husband, George, and their two cats.

Joan Holub is the author and/or illustrator of many books for children. You can find out more about Joan and her books on her Web site, *www.joanholub.com*.

Doll Hospital™
Paper Dolls

Add to your Doll Hospital™ paper doll collection with
an adorable Marissa paper doll and three beautiful outfits,
available on *www.scholastic.com/titles/dollhospital*.

At *www.scholastic.com/titles/dollhospital*
you'll also learn all about the dolls of Doll Hospital™,
read fun stories about dolls, and get to know
the author of Doll Hospital™, Joan Holub.

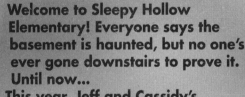